the little red fish

taeeun yoo

Dial Books for Young Readers

To my grandfather Heungno Yoo and my niece, Sohyung

DIAL BOOKS FOR YOUNG READERS
A division of Penguin Young Readers Group •Published by The Penguin Group
Penguin Group (USA) Inc., 375 Hudson Street, New York, NY 10014, U.S.A. • Penguin Group (Canada),
90 Eglinton Avenue East, Suite 700, Toronto, Ontario, Canada M4P 2Y3 (a division of Pearson Penguin
Canada Inc.) •Penguin Books Ltd, 80 Strand, London WC2R 0RL, England • Penguin Ireland, 25 St.
Stephen's Green, Dublin 2, Ireland (a division of Penguin Books Ltd) • Penguin Group (Australia), 250
Camberwell Road, Camberwell, Victoria 3124, Australia (a division of Pearson Australia Group Pty
Ltd) • Penguin Books India Pvt Ltd, 11 Community Centre, Panchsheel Park, New Delhi - 110 017,
India •Penguin Group (NZ), Cnr Airborne and Rosedale Roads, Albany, Auckland 1310, New Zealand
(a division of Pearson New Zealand Ltd) •Penguin Books (South Africa) (Pty) Ltd, 24 Sturdee Avenue,
Rosebank, Johannesburg 2196, South Africa • Penguin Books Ltd, Registered Offices: 80 Strand, London
WC2R 0RL, England

Designed by Lily Malcom
Text set in Hiroshige
Manufactured in China on acid-free paper

10 9 8 7 6 5 4 3 2 1

CIP available upon request

The art was created using etching and hand color

JeJe's grandfather was a librarian at an old library in the middle of the forest. One day he allowed JeJe to come along with him, and JeJe brought his friend the little red fish.

It was the first time JeJe had ever been allowed to go inside
and he was amazed by all the different rooms filled with books.
He explored from one corner to another.

Soon he grew tired and fell asleep.

When JeJe opened his eyes, the room was dark and quiet. He felt as though he had been swallowed up by the darkness.

Scared and lonely, JeJe sat near the light of the moon and began reading a book to his little red fish. But when he looked up, the fish was gone!

JeJe began to search for his fish, from bookshelf to bookshelf and room to room. He caught a glimpse of a little red tail flipping high over a shelf and so he followed it.

He almost caught the fish, but it disappeared again near an old book layered with dust. Could that be his fish's tail peeking out of the middle of the book? Jeje picked it up, and when he opened it . . . something magical happened.

All of the fish looked the same. Which one was his?
JeJe realized that his fish was hiding in the book! He
reached down to catch it and as he tried, he fell down,
down into the page.

Back in the library, JeJe opened his hands, and there was his little red fish looking up at him. He gently returned it back into its bowl.

JeJe placed the red book back on the shelf and took his little red fish home. He whispered to his fish that they would come back to the library very soon.